My Weird School Special

Back to School, Weird Kids Rule!

Dan Gutman
Pictures by
Jim Paillot

HARPER
An Imprint of HarperCollinsPublishers

To Jules Boyle and Alex Soumilas

My Weird School Special: Back to School, Weird Kids Rule!

Text copyright © 2014 by Dan Gutman

Illustrations copyright © 2014 by Jim Paillot

Library of Congress Control Number: 2013953793

ISBN 978-0-06-220685-5 (trade bdg.) — ISBN 978-0-06-220686-2 (lib. bdg.)

Typography by Kate Engbring

14 15 16 17 18 OPM 10 9 8 7 6 5 4 3 2 1

❖

First Edition

Contents

My Side of the Story

My name is Andrea and I love school!

Ha! I bet you were expecting this story would be told by my boyfriend and future husband, A.J. Well, think again, silly! Arlo (that's his *real* name) and his family are on summer vacation in Bermuda. They're not coming back until next week, when school starts. So now it's *my* turn. Finally,

I get to tell *my* side of the story.

This is going to be *fun*! I even got a special notebook to write in. I love writing. Don't you? (Oh, I guess you can't answer that question because you're on *that* side of the book and I'm on *this* side.)

Aren't parentheses fun? (Answer yes or no here.) I love parentheses because I can pretend that I'm whispering into somebody's ear (like this).

Let's get started!

Aren't exclamation points fun? I love exclamation points because I can pretend that I'm shouting (LIKE THIS!). Exclamation points are sort of like the opposite of parentheses. The more exclamation points

you use, the louder you can shout!!!!!!!!!!!!!!
(See?)

I like question marks, too. (Don't you?????)

In general, I'm a big fan of punctuation. (Can you tell?)

Anyway, as I was saying, I love school. School is cool. You can't spell "SCHOOL" without "COOL," right? The only thing I don't like about school is that we can't go there during the summer.

Do you know the reason why we don't go to school in the summer? It's because a long time ago when most kids lived on farms, they had to help out in the fields during July and August. I know that's true because I looked it up in my encyclopedia. (I love looking up stuff.) Most of us don't live on farms these days, so we should really go to school all year round, if you ask me.

Anyway, back to the story . . .

Ding-dong!

Oh, wait. Hang on a second. Somebody just rang the doorbell. That's weird. It's nighttime. Why would somebody be coming over to my house *now*? I'll be right back.

"I'll get it, Mom!" I shouted.

"Who could that be at this hour?" my mom asked.

Well, you'll never believe who rang the doorbell.

It was Arlo!

★

The #1 reason why I love school . . . Our wonderful teachers!

I love teachers because they are so nice to devote their lives to children (not even their own children!). Maybe I'll be a teacher when I grow up. Or maybe I'll be a veterinarian.

Or a singer. Or a dancer.

Maybe I'll be a singing and dancing veterinarian who teaches in her spare time! I'm really not sure what I want to be when I grow up. But I don't have to decide that right now, do I?

If you ask me, a teacher should win the Nobel Prize. That's a prize they give out to people who do something good for the world.

What, you thought it was for something else?

★

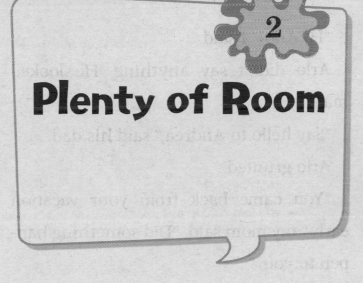

Plenty of Room

When I opened the door, Arlo and his family were standing on our front porch. My mom and Arlo's mom are best friends. They started hugging because they haven't seen each other in two whole weeks. I hid my notebook behind my back. Arlo might be mad if he knew I was writing this.

"Hi Arlo!" I said.

Arlo didn't say anything. He looked mad.

"Say hello to Andrea," said his dad.

Arlo grunted.

"You came back from your vacation early," my mom said. "Did something happen to you?"

"There was a hurricane in Bermuda," Arlo's dad told us. "It was pretty bad."

"Hurricanes usually form over large bodies of warm water," I told everybody. "The water evaporates and turns into clouds when moist air rises and cools."

(I knew that because I looked it up in my encyclopedia.)

Arlo rolled his eyes.

"It was scary!" said his sister, Amy.

"They told everybody to evacuate."

Arlo started giggling.

"What's so funny?" I asked him.

"Amy just said they told everybody to evacuate."

"So?"

"'Evacuate' is a fancy word for pooping!" Arlo said.

"It is not," I told him.

"Is too."

"I'll look it up in my encyclopedia," I said. "That will prove you're wrong."

"Go ahead," Arlo replied. "Look it up in your dumb encyclopedia."

I got my encyclopedia, which has a built-in dictionary. It's really cool because it's electronic. All you need to do is say a word, and a second later the encyclopedia tells you the definition out loud.

"Evac-u-ate," I told the encyclopedia.

"*To discharge from the body as waste,*" the encyclopedia replied.

"See, I *told* you 'evacuate' means pooping," said Arlo.

Oooh, I *hate* it when Arlo is right!

"You are *so* immature!" I shouted. "And disgusting!"

"Your *face* is disgusting," Arlo replied.

"Stop arguing!" shouted Arlo's mom. "I wish you two would get along better."

My parents invited Arlo's parents inside to have coffee, because that's what grown-ups do. I poured juice for Arlo and Amy.

"Didn't you rent out your house while you were away?" my dad asked Arlo's dad.

"Yeah, we can't go back there for a week," Arlo's dad said. "We just stopped by to let you know we're home. We're on our way to a hotel tonight. I booked a room for the week."

"Hotel?!" my mother shouted. "Don't be silly! That will cost you a lot of money. You're staying here with us."

"WHAT?!" Arlo shouted.

"Oh, there isn't enough room," said

Arlo's mom. "We don't want to be a bother."

"It's a great idea!" I said. "Arlo and I will have fun together!"

"I vote for the hotel," said Arlo.

"We have *plenty* of room," my mom insisted. "There's the guest bedroom for the grown-ups. Amy can sleep in my office."

"What about me?" Arlo asked.

"We'll put a sleeping bag on the floor in Andrea's room for you," said my mom.

"WHAT?!" Arlo shouted.

★

The #2 reason why I love school . . . School has rules!

Rules are important. If we didn't have rules, the boys would misbehave and shoot spitballs and cut in line and shout things out without raising their hands first. Because that's what boys do. And the next thing you know, all the boys would be running wild in the streets and doing disgusting boy things like burping the alphabet and making armpit farts. That's why it's really important to have rules and for everybody to follow them. Especially boys.

★

Boys Are Weird

I helped Arlo bring his stuff in from the car.

"This is going to be fun!" I told him as we climbed the stairs. "We can have a slumber party!"

Arlo grunted again. When we got to my room, he covered his eyes like he was shielding them from the sun.

"So much *pink*," he moaned. "It's blinding me!"

"Very *funny*, Arlo," I said.

"What are you hiding behind your back?" he asked after he uncovered his eyes.

"Oh, nothing important," I told him. "Just my secret diary. It's not for you to read."

"I don't *want* to read your dumb diary," he said.

"Good," I told him. "Because you *can't*. You're not allowed. It's *secret*."

"Well, if you won't let me read it, then I want to," Arlo said. He snatched the notebook out of my hand.

"Hey, give that back,
Arlo!" I shouted.

I tried to get my notebook away from

him, but he wouldn't give it to me. He sat on the floor in the corner and started reading it. There was nothing I could do. I unrolled a sleeping bag on the floor.

After a few minutes, Arlo closed my notebook.

"First of all," he said, "I'm *not* your boy-friend. I'm not even your *friend*. I'm your sworn enemy for life."

Arlo is always saying things like that to me. But I know he doesn't mean them. My mother is a psychologist, and she told me that when a boy really likes a girl, he will say he *doesn't* like her. That's what boys do. And the more they say they don't like you, the more they really *like* you. So obviously, Arlo is in love with me.

Boys are weird.

"Who wants a toasted marshmallow?" my dad hollered from downstairs.

"I do!" Arlo and I hollered back. (Who *doesn't* like toasted marshmallows?)

We ran downstairs. Our dads had fired up the grill in the backyard and gave each of us a really long stick so we could toast marshmallows.

Arlo stuck his marshmallow right into the fire, and then he waved it around like a torch.

"Look! I'm in the Olympics," he said, running around the backyard. Then he slid the blackened marshmallow off his stick and ate it. Ugh, gross!

"You're eating pure carbon, you know," I told him.

"Carbon tastes great!"

I slowly turned my marshmallow until it was golden brown on all sides. It took a few minutes to make it perfect. By the time I was finished toasting my marshmallow, Arlo had already eaten three or four of his burned carbon balls.

We toasted a bunch of marshmallows, and then our parents said it was getting close to bedtime. Arlo and I went upstairs.

"I have a *great* idea!" I said. "Let's tell ghost stories!"

"I'm tired," Arlo said as he climbed into the sleeping bag.

"Aren't you going to brush your teeth?" I asked.

"No," he grunted.

"If you don't brush your teeth regularly,

you'll get cavities," I told him. "Your teeth might even fall out."

"Can you stop talking now?" Arlo said. "I'm trying to sleep."

"Did you ever hear of gingivitis?" I asked him. "That's a disease where your gums get inflamed."

"I don't think my gums are gonna catch on fire," Arlo grunted from inside the sleeping bag.

"I brush my teeth seven times a day so I won't get gingivitis," I told him. "Once when I wake up, once after breakfast, once before lunch, once after lunch, once before dinner, once after dinner, and once at bedtime. And of course I floss and use mouthwash every day too. You should really pay attention to your dental hygiene, Arlo. *Arlo?*"

I looked down at the floor. Arlo was asleep.

★

The #3 reason why I love school . . . There's no TV at school.

TV is filled with shows about people eating worms and beating each other up and shooting guns and acting mean. That's not very nice, and it's a bad influence on children. No wonder people in the real world beat each other up, shoot guns, act mean, and eat worms.

Do you know what my favorite week of the year is? TV Turnoff Week.

★

The Ghost

I don't know how long I was sleeping. But sometime in the middle of the night, I heard something moving in my room. And then I heard an eerie voice.

"Andrea . . . Andrea . . ."

I was in a deep sleep. I had forgotten that Arlo was sleeping on my floor. I just heard that creepy voice. When I opened my eyes, there was a big, shapeless creature standing next to my bed and scary shadows on the wall behind it.

"*Eeeeeeeeeeek!*" I screamed.

Then I realized it was just Arlo. He had the sleeping bag over his head.

"Andrea . . . Andrea . . ."

"Knock it off, Arlo!" I told him. "I'm trying to sleep."

"I'm not Arlo," he replied. "I'm the *ghost* of Arlo."

"Oh, yeah?" I said. "If you're the ghost of Arlo, that must mean Arlo is dead."

"That's right," he said. "He ran away to Antarctica to live with the penguins. But

he fell off an ice floe and froze to death. It was tragic."

I decided to play along.

"What's your name?" I asked.

"Name?" he said. "My name is . . . the ghost of Arlo."

"That's not a name," I told him. "You're supposed to have a name. Ghosts have names."

"How do you know what ghosts are supposed to have?" Arlo said. "Have you ever met a ghost?"

"This is silly, Arlo! Take the sleeping bag off your head. You almost scared me to death."

"You *should* be scared," Arlo said in a

scary voice. "After you go to sleep, I'm going to paint your pink room black."

"You are not."

"Yes, and I'm going to hide under your bed," Arlo said. "And when you go to sleep, I'm going to replace your Barbies with G.I. Joe action figures. Because that's what Arlo would do. If he was still alive. Which he isn't."

"Don't you dare touch my Barbies," I warned him.

"Then I'm going to take away your encyclopedia," Arlo said. "And I'm going to change all your As to Fs on your next report card."

"Go to sleep," I told him. "There's no

such thing as ghosts. You're Arlo."

"I am not."

"Are too!"

"R2D2."

At that moment, the door opened.

"*Eeeeeeeeeek!*" Arlo and I screamed.

It was Arlo's dad and my dad.

"We heard a noise," Arlo's dad said. "Is

everything okay?"

"I'm dead," Arlo said. "This is my ghost."

"Go to sleep!" they both shouted. And then they slammed the door.

★

The #4 reason why I love school . . . We get to learn new things!

Learning new things is fun. But more importantly, it makes the world a better place. The more you know, the better you are.

Last year for Christmas I got my electronic encyclopedia. It's like a paper encyclopedia except that you can jump around from topic to topic just by clicking on words. I like to look things up in the encyclopedia for fun. You never know what you might find.

The other day I looked up "gopher" in my encyclopedia. While I was reading about gophers, I clicked on a link to pests. I started reading that, and then I clicked on a link to germs. That looked really interesting, too, so I started reading it. There was a link to cheese, so I clicked on it.

Did you know that there are four-thousand-year-old pictures of cheese in Egyptian tombs? I never would have learned that if I hadn't looked up "gopher."

★

Agree to
Disagree

When we woke up the next morning, I could smell the yummy smell of waffles cooking. I *love* waffles! Arlo and I ran downstairs. We got to pour the batter. When you help make the waffles, it makes them taste even yummier.

"You kids go play," my mom told us

after we finished. "A.J.'s mom and I will have coffee."

Grown-ups sure love coffee. They drink it *all* the time. At school one day the coffee machine broke down, and the teachers were walking around like zombies because they didn't have their morning coffee.

I tasted coffee once. It was yucky. But when I'm a grown-up, I'll force myself to drink it, because that's the rule. I always follow the rules.

"What do you want to play?" I asked Arlo.

"I don't know," he said. "What do *you* want to play?"

"Too bad we can't start working on our homework to get a jump on it," I told Arlo.

...Need COFFEE...

"I know! We can finish our
summer reading!"

"WHAT?!" Arlo exclaimed. "It's
summer! I hate reading! We have to read
all year long. I don't even like reading

street signs during the summer. They should have summer *not* reading."

"Do you want to play dress-up?" I asked Arlo. (I *love* playing dress-up!)

"No!"

I realized that Arlo was just going to say no to anything I suggested. Because that's what boys do. So I came up with a plan to make him say yes.

"Do you want to play with my Barbies?" I asked.

"No!" Arlo replied. "Boys don't play with Barbies."

"That's just what grown-ups *tell* you," I said to Arlo. "Are you going to let a bunch of grown-ups tell you what you can or can't do? That doesn't sound like you,

Arlo. A man like you makes up your *own* mind, right?"

I was using psychology to get Arlo to play with my Barbies. My mom taught me how to do that. She's really smart because she went to Harvard.

"Okay, okay," Arlo agreed. "Get out your dumb Barbies."

"Yay!"

I got my Barbie collection out of my closet. I have Ice Capades Barbie, Angel Princess Barbie, and Halloween Glow Barbie (with a glow-in-the-dark hair extension).

"Can we cut their heads off?" Arlo asked.

"Of course not!" I said.

"Can we go outside and melt their faces

with a magnifying glass?" Arlo asked.

"Absolutely not!"

"Can we throw them out the window and see what happens when they hit the ground?" Arlo asked.

"No!"

"Then I don't want to play with your Barbies."

"That's not fair!" I told Arlo. "You said you'd play with them."

"Cutting their heads off, melting their faces, and throwing them out the window *is* playing with them," Arlo said.

"It is not!"

"It is too."

"I'll tell you what," I told Arlo. "Let's agree to disagree."

"No," Arlo replied.

"You won't even agree to disagree?" I asked.

"The only thing I agree with is that you're wrong," he replied.

This was not going well. I would have to use more psychology.

"Arlo, if you won't agree to disagree with me, that must mean you agree with me."

Arlo thought about that for a moment.

"I disagree with *that*," he said.

"Now you're just being obnoxious, Arlo!"

"I am not!"

"Stop fighting!" my mother called from downstairs. "Get ready, you two, because we have to go."

"Go where?" Arlo and I asked.

"We need to go shopping for back-to-school clothes," shouted Arlo's mom.

"Yay!" I said. "I *love* shopping for back-to-school clothes!"

"Boo!" Arlo said. "I hate shopping for back-to-school clothes!"

★

The #5 reason why I love school . . .

It gives me a good education!

Getting a good education will help me become the high school valedictorian. Do you know what a valedictorian is? She is the student who gets the best grades in the whole school. I want to be high school valedictorian because it will help me get into Harvard. My mom went there, and look at her! Going to Harvard will help me get a good job someday.

I have it all planned out. When you plan everything out, there are no unpleasant surprises.

★

First Impressions Count

Shopping is fun! And I don't think there's anything in the world that I love more than shopping for *clothes*. Think of it—if we didn't shop for clothes, we would be walking around naked all the time. Ewww, gross!

We piled into my mom's minivan and drove to the mall, where they have this store called Macy's. It's a department store. That's a store that has lots of different departments, so it has the perfect name.

When we walked inside, Arlo looked like we were taking him to his own funeral.

"Don't you want to look handsome for the first day of school?" I asked him.

"No."

Arlo and his mom went off to the boys' department, and my mom and I went to the girls' department.

There were so many important decisions to be made. Should I get a long, flowy skirt, or should I get a skort? (That's a skirt with shorts underneath.) Should I get pleather pants (that's fake leather), or should I get jeggings? (Those are leggings that look like jeans.) The outfit that I wear on the first day of school is crucial, because first impressions count.

I picked out a bunch of things and went

into the fitting room. I tried on a short skirt, a long skirt, and a high-low skirt. Then I came out and looked in the mirror with my mom to decide which things looked the best on me.

A few minutes after we started shopping, I saw Arlo and his mom coming over to the girls' department. They were carrying a bunch of bags.

"You're done *already*?" my mom asked.

"He's a *boy*," said Arlo's mom. "We finished half an hour ago."

"Can we leave now?" Arlo asked.

"Leave?" we all said. "We're just getting *started*!"

Someday, when Arlo and I are married,

I'll get him to dress up in nice clothes. He will look so handsome. But for now I couldn't worry about Arlo. I had important shopping decisions to make.

I tried on a fringed crop top with rhinestones on it. I came out of the fitting room and spun around so Arlo could get the full effect.

"What do you think of *this*?" I asked.

"I hate it."

"Oh, you're just saying that to tease me," I told him. "You really love it, right?"

"No, I really hate it."

"I think you really mean the opposite," I told him.

"You're right. I really love it," Arlo said.

"You mean you hate it?" I asked.

I wasn't sure if Arlo was using psychology on me or not.

Shopping for clothes takes a *long* time. Poor Arlo was really bored. But what was I supposed to do? You don't want to make a mistake and get stuck with clothes you'll

never wear. I got a nice rainbow dress for Picture Day. And just for the fun of it, I got a pair of pink sunglasses and a bathing suit with butterflies on it to wear at the beach.

"I picked out all my outfits for the first two weeks of school," I told Arlo. "I don't like waiting until the last minute."

"Then why don't you start planning your funeral *now*?" he said.

"Very funny. Oh, look, Arlo! They even have little fuzzy purses that look like kittens! Isn't that adorable? I wonder if my mom would let me buy one."

I turned around. Arlo wasn't there.

"Arlo?"

I walked around the rack of Hello Kitty shirts. He wasn't there either.

"Arlo!" I shouted.

He wasn't *anywhere*!

"Arlo is gone!"

"WHAT?!" both of our moms yelled.

"One minute he was right next to me," I explained, "and the next minute he disappeared!"

"Maybe he went to the bathroom," said my mom.

Arlo's mom started screaming and crying and freaking out.

"My son is missing!" she shouted. "A.J.! Where are you? Somebody lock the doors! My son is gone!"

An alarm sounded, and security guards came running over. Everybody was searching all over the store for Arlo.

Finally, about five minutes later, we found him. He was hiding inside a big round rack of fake-fur vests.

"A.J.! What are you doing in there?" his mom shouted. "I thought you had been kidnapped!"

"I was pretending this was an army fort, and I was hiding out from the enemy," he said. "What's the big deal?"

Arlo's mom put her hands on her hips, so I knew she was really mad. But I think she was holding it in because she didn't want to yell at Arlo in front of everybody.

"Andrea and I are just about done here," my mom said. "I'll go pay for these things. Then we need to have lunch and go shopping for back-to-school supplies."

"Yay!" I shouted. "I *love* shopping for back-to-school supplies!"

"Boo!" Arlo shouted. "I hate shopping for back-to-school supplies!"

★

The #6 reason why I love school . . .

We get delicious, nutritious cafeteria food!

Our lunch lady, Ms. LaGrange, always prepares lots of healthy options so we'll grow up to be big and strong. Arlo and his friends are always stuffing themselves with junk food and sugary drinks, but not me. Maybe I'll become a vegetarian when I grow up.

★

The Buddy System

We piled back into the minivan and stopped off for lunch (Pizza! Yum!), and then we drove to my favorite store in the whole world—Staples!

I *love* Staples because they have rows and rows of pens and pencils and glue sticks and highlighters and notebooks and rubber bands and paper clips and everything else students need to do well in school. (They even sell staples!) Our school sent out a list of supplies we would need this year.

There was a big sign on the front of Staples that said BACK-TO-SCHOOL SALE.

Staples is *huge*. When we got out of the minivan, our moms said Arlo and I had to use the buddy system to make sure that *one* of us (guess who?) didn't get lost in the store again.

"You kids need to stay together at *all* times," my mom told us. "Do you understand?"

"Yes!" I said.

Arlo grunted.

"And to be safe," Arlo's mom said, "I

want you to hold hands."

"WHAT?" Arlo shouted. "I'm not hold-ing hands with a girl!"

"A.J.!" said Arlo's mom with her hands on her hips.

Arlo held my hand.

"Let's skip!" I said.

"No!"

When we stepped on the rubber door-mat and the front door of Staples slid open, it was almost like I could hear angels singing. There were school sup-plies as far as the eye could see! Crayons and calculators and clipboards and hole punchers and scissors and rulers and tape and glitter glue and Post-it notes in lots of

different colors, shapes, and sizes.

"I could spend all day here," I said.

Our moms went to look at the office furniture. They told us again that we had to stay together and hold hands at all times.

We got a shopping cart. Someday, when Arlo and I are married, we'll go shopping together just like this, except that Arlo will sit on a bench outside and wait for me to finish. That's what husbands do.

"Where should we go first?" I asked Arlo.

"Home," he replied.

"Let's look at pens!" I said, because pens are something you need every day at school.

When we got to the pen aisle, a funny-looking man came over to us.

"May I help you?" he asked.

"We need to buy pens for school," I said.

"You're in luck," he said. "My name is Mr. Debakey. I'm a pen specialist."

A *pen* specialist? I never heard of a pen specialist. Mr. Debakey took a little box out of his pocket.

"May I suggest this Montblanc Meisterstück Classique writing instrument?" he said. "It's been engineered for precise handling and comfort, and it features a reliable swivel mechanism. As you can see, it has a beautiful jet-black finish with twenty-three-carat, gold-plated trim."

"Wow," I said. "How much does it cost?"

"Three hundred and fifty-seven dollars."

"Three hundred and fifty-seven dollars for a *pen*?" Arlo shouted. "You gotta be joking."

"I never joke about pens," said Mr. Debakey.

"Look, we just need some plain old pens, okay?" said Arlo. "Nothing fancy."

Mr. Debakey looked disappointed.

"Fine," he said. "I believe a pen must be carefully matched to its user. I want you to be happy with your pen selection. So tell me, do you want ballpoint, gel, or felt-tip pens?"

"Ballpoint," I said.

"Do you want disposable or replaceable ink cartridge?"

"Disposable," I said.

"Retractable point?"

"No."

"Fine point, extra-fine point, or medium point?"

"Fine."

"Blue, black, red, or green ink?"

"Blue."

"Paper Mate or BIC?"

"They're just *pens*!" Arlo shouted, rolling his eyes. "It doesn't matter! This is dumb!"

"Calm down, Arlo," I told him. "You're causing a scene."

"Young man, I've spent my whole life studying pens," said Mr. Debakey. "Did you know that the ballpoint pen was invented by a Massachusetts man named John J. Loud back in 1888?"

"Who cares?" said Arlo.

"You sure know a lot about pens, Mr. Debakey," I said.

"Pens are my life."

"Let's get out of here," Arlo whispered into my ear. "Mr. Debakey is flaky."

Arlo was probably right. I said good-bye to Mr. Debakey and pushed the cart away from him.

"Perhaps you need some pencils?" asked Mr. Debakey as he followed us down the aisle.

"Not today, thank you," I said.

"Personally, I prefer new pencils with erasers at the end," Mr. Debakey said, "because that means nobody has ever made a mistake with them. It's sad when a pencil has its eraser all worn down. That means somebody has made a *lot* of mistakes. I don't like making mistakes."

"We don't want any pencils!" Arlo shouted back at him. "Leave us alone!"

As we walked away, Mr. Debakey started crying.

"Come back!" he sobbed. "There's a lot more I need to tell you about writing implements!"

Mr. Debakey was weird. We ran down the pencil-and-pen aisle with our cart and turned the corner to go into the next aisle.

You'll never believe who we saw there.

It was our friends Michael and Ryan!

They were with their moms. When he saw Michael and Ryan, Arlo tried to let go of my hand, but I held on tight because our moms told us to. I always follow the rules.

"*Oooooh!*" Ryan said. "A.J. and Andrea are holding hands while they buy back-to-school supplies together. They must be in *love!*"

"When are you gonna get married?" asked Michael.

"We are *not* in love!" Arlo yelled. "We are *never* going to get married! Stop saying that!"

"Calm down, Arlo," I said. "You're getting hysterical."

Ryan and Michael started singing that song that goes "A.J. and Andrea sitting in a tree, K-I-S-S-I-N-G."

Arlo looked like he was going to explode.

★

The #7 reason why I love school . . .
Taking classes after school!

What's more fun than going to school? More school, of course! After school is over, I take art classes and music classes and dancing classes and lots of other classes. I even took a class in juggling. Learning is fun. I wonder if it's possible to learn so much that your head explodes. I'm going to look that up in my encyclopedia.

★

Arguing with Arlo

We spent a long time going up and down every aisle at Staples. Our cart was almost filled to the top. These are some of the things I picked out . . .

- a box of crayons (with a built-in crayon sharpener!)

- a new cork bulletin board for my room
- a school year calendar
- a bunch of Book Sox (They're like socks for your books!)
- a lunch box with Cray-Z on it (He's my favorite singer.)
- a bottle of hand sanitizer (because I don't want to get everybody else's germs)
- two-pocket folders with pictures of kittens on them (I almost picked the ones with bunnies, but the kittens were cuter.)
- erasers (but I don't need many of those because I hardly ever make mistakes)
- a name badge (so it will be easier for everybody to remember my name on

the first day of school)

- a notepad in the shape of a cupcake (It's adorable!)
- a plastic organizer for my desk drawer (I love organizing things. It's fun to put different school supplies into separate containers.)
- a new backpack
- a tape dispenser (in the shape of a high-heeled shoe!)
- oh, and a box of staples (I couldn't forget them!)

"Look, Arlo!" I said. "They even sell laminating sheets! We can laminate things at home. Isn't that exciting?"

"This place is a snoozefest," said Arlo.

"Can we get out of here now?"

Boys just don't understand shopping.

We found our moms, and they paid for the school supplies. When we got home, Arlo parked himself in front of the TV (of course). I went to my room to organize my things.

First I removed all the tags from the clothes I bought and hung the clothes neatly in my closet. I organized the outfits in the order of which one I would wear on each day of the week for the first two weeks of school.

Next I lined up all my school supplies in alphabetical order. (Lining things up is fun.) Then I put all the school supplies into separate containers and stuck labels on them so I would know what was inside each one.

I was all ready for the first day of school. My new clothes were hanging up. My school supplies were ready to go. My bedroom was neat and clean. I even looked up a bunch of words in the dictionary just in case I would need to know those words for the new school year.

There wasn't anything else to do except sit around and wait for school to start. I went downstairs. Arlo was in the living room playing video games.

"Is that all you ever do?" I asked him. "Watch TV and play video games?"

"I *like* watching TV and playing video games," he said. "It's fun. Your problem is, you don't know how to have fun."

"I do too!" I told him. "I have *lots* of fun."

"Yeah, you have fun organizing your school supplies."

(Actually, I *do* have fun organizing my school supplies. But I didn't want to admit that.)

I was tired of arguing with Arlo all the time. I went into the kitchen, where my mom and Arlo's mom were drinking coffee (of course) and whispering to each other. They stopped whispering when they saw me.

"What are you whispering about?" I asked them.

"Oh, nothing," they said really quickly.

"I'm bored," I told them.

"Why don't you and A.J. go out to play?" said Arlo's mom.

"What?!" Arlo yelled from the living room. "You mean play *outside*? Are you *crazy*? We could get hit by a car out there. Or get kidnapped. Or sunburned. Or a tree could fall on our heads. You don't know *what* might happen. It's dangerous out there!"

"Don't be silly, Arlo," I told him. "We could play hopscotch."

"Hopscotch is for girls."

"We could jump rope," I suggested.

"Jumping rope is for girls."

"It is not," I told Arlo. "Professional boxers jump rope all the time to get in shape for their fights."

"They do not."

"Do too."

"Stop arguing all the time!" Arlo's mom shouted. "You two sound like an old married couple!"

Arlo and I were definitely getting on each other's nerves. We *all* were. It's hard for two families to live in one small house. Maybe Arlo's family should have stayed in a hotel after all.

One time my mom told me about an experiment where some psychologists put a bunch of rats in a cage that was too small for them. After a while the rats started getting sick, attacking each other, and eating their own children! Eww, gross!

I certainly didn't want that to happen in our house. I would just have to try and get along with Arlo the best I could.

"So what do you want to do?" I asked him politely.

"Let's watch TV."

"TV is boring," I said. "Let's read a book together."

"Reading books is boring," Arlo said. "Let's play video games."

"Playing video games is boring," I told him. "Let's sing a song."

"Singing songs is boring."

"It is not!" I yelled.

"Your *face* is boring."

"Mom!" I shouted. "Arlo is being mean to me again!"

"She hurt my feelings!" Arlo whined.

"Oh, come on, Arlo," I told him. "You don't have feelings."

"I do too," he said. "When I fell off my bike last week, I felt it."

"Stop fighting!" my mom shouted. "You kids are driving us *crazy*!"

"That's it!" said Arlo's mom. "That's the last straw!"

"What do straws have to do with

anything?" Arlo asked.

"We can't take it anymore!" his mom shouted. "We're sending the two of you to day camp for the rest of the summer."

"WHAT?!" Arlo shouted.

★

The #8 reason why I love school . . .

I get to see my friends!

Emily has been my best friend since we were in preschool together. We go everywhere and do everything together. Arlo and his friends tease her sometimes. But I would never do that because that's not what friends do.

★

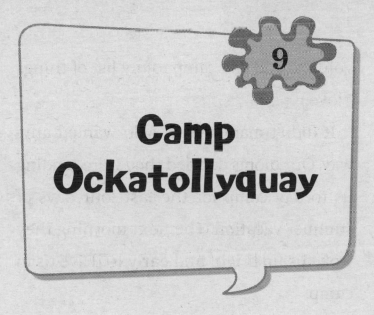

Camp Ockatollyquay

9

"Day camp?" Arlo shouted. "We don't want to go to day camp!"

"Speak for yourself, Arlo," I told him. "Maybe *I* want to go to day camp."

I used to go to day camp when I was little. We got to play sports and sing songs and go swimming and put on plays and make lanyards and pottery. I loved it! (I'm going to add day camp to my list of things I love.)

It didn't matter what Arlo wanted anyway. Our moms decided they were sending us to day camp for the last four days of summer vacation. The next morning they woke us up bright and early to drive us to camp.

Our moms sat in the front seat. They looked really happy. Arlo and I sat in the backseat. He was scowling the whole time. I checked to make sure my bathing suit, notebook, camera, and other things were properly organized in my backpack.

It took about a half an hour until we pulled into the parking lot at Camp Ockatollyquay. That's what the sign said. I guess it's a Native American name or something.

"Bye! Have fun!" my mom shouted when we got out of the car. "Don't forget to put on sunscreen!"

"We'll pick you up at the end of the day," said Arlo's mom.

They peeled out of the parking lot in a cloud of dust. They were probably going to go drink more coffee.

A lady came out of the office. Well, she was really just a teenager. She had on thick glasses and was carrying a clipboard.

"You must be Andrea and A.J.," she said. "My name is Miss Janey. Welcome to Camp Ockatollyquay. I'm going to be your counselor. Follow me. Let's go find

the rest of our group."

Miss Janey was nice. I loved her already. She led us past the soccer field and the swimming pool toward a big building at the other end of the camp.

"How come there's no water in the swimming pool?" Arlo asked.

"Oh, we don't use the swimming pool," said Miss Janey.

"How come there are no kids playing on the soccer field?" I asked.

"Oh, we don't use the soccer field," said Miss Janey.

"Are we going to play sports and sing songs and put on plays and make lanyards and pottery?" I asked.

"No, we don't do those things at Camp Ockatollyquay," said Miss Janey.

"This camp is weird," Arlo whispered to me.

Miss Janey opened the door of the building and led us down the hall to a room.

And you'll never believe who was in there.

It was our friends Emily, Michael, Ryan, Alexia, and Neil! The whole gang was there! And they were all wearing pajamas! Emily gave me a big hug when she saw me.

"Oooh," Ryan said. "A.J. and Andrea came to camp together. They must be in *love."*

"When are you gonna get married?" asked Michael.

"We *had* to come here together," Arlo told them. "My family is living in her house all week."

"*Oooh,* A.J. is living in Andrea's house," said Ryan. "They must be in *love.*"

"When are you gonna get married?" asked Michael.

"Well, I see you kids are already friends," said Miss Janey. "I need to let the office know where we are. I'll be back in a few minutes."

Miss Janey ran off.

"What are *you* guys doing here?" Arlo asked. "And why are you wearing your pajamas?"

"It's Pajama Day," said Alexia. "Every day is a different weird day here."

"Our parents couldn't stand us any-more," said Neil. "So they shipped us off to day camp."

"Same with us!" Arlo told them.

"All the cool day camps were filled up already," said Ryan. "This is the only one that had room for us the last week of sum-mer vacation."

"You gotta get us out of here, A.J.!" begged Michael. "This place is *horrible*!"

"What's so horrible about it?" Arlo asked.

"It's a—"

Michael didn't get the chance to finish his sentence, because that's when Miss Janey came back.

"I hear that you two are in the gifted and talented program at your school," she

said to Arlo and me. "Well, I think you're going to *love* Camp Ockatollyquay!"

I had heard of sports camps and chess camps and tennis camps and computer camps and even camps for kids who are overweight.

"What kind of a camp *is* this?" I asked Miss Janey.

"You mean your parents didn't tell you?" she replied. "Camp Ockatollyquay is a back-to-school camp. We're going to get you ready for the school year."

Arlo fainted.

★

The #9 reason why I love school . . . We get to take tests!

Tests are fun. They also help us understand what we don't know so we can learn those things and do better on the next test. I try to get all the answers right on tests so that I will become the high school valedictorian and get into Harvard someday.

★

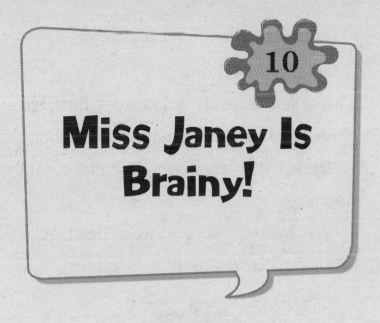

Miss Janey Is Brainy!

Arlo was flat on his back with his eyes closed.

"Somebody get the camp doctor!" Miss Janey shouted.

"Do you want me to give Arlo mouth-to-mouth resuscitation?" I asked. "I took a CPR class last year—"

"I don't think that will be necessary,

Andrea," she said.

In a few seconds Arlo's eyes fluttered open. We all picked him up off the floor.

"Dude, you were totally *out*!" said Alexia.

"You looked like you were dead, A.J.," said Ryan. "It was *cool*!"

"I was having a dream," Arlo mumbled. "There were these penguins. They wanted me to come with them to Antarctica."

"You'll be fine," said Miss Janey. "We need to get back to work. There are only a few days left before school starts, and we have so much to accomplish."

"Let me get this straight," Arlo said. "This camp is sort of like . . . *school*?"

"Exactly!" said Miss Janey. "You're going to have so much fun when we do the Math Olympics, and Vocabulary Volleyball, and Science Challenge, and Social Studies—"

"You gotta be kidding me," Arlo said.

"I *told* you," said Michael. "They should call this place Torture Camp."

"Well, I think back-to-school camp is

a *great* idea!" I said. "I love learning new things. And you can never be too prepared for school."

"I agree," said Emily.

"*That's* the spirit!" said Miss Janey. "Let's get to work!"

For the rest of the morning, Miss Janey gave us reading drills and spelling drills and math drills and history drills and just about every other kind of drill you could think up. It was fun! She knows so much about every subject in the world.

Miss Janey is brainy!

The next day at camp was Crazy Clothes Day, where everybody had to dress up in silly clothes. I wore a pink baseball cap that had a little propeller on the top. We spent a lot of time doing math drills.

The day after that was Purple Day, where everybody had to wear something purple. I wore a purple scarf, and we spent the whole day learning about geography and volcanoes and neat things like that.

I was sad that the next day was going to be the last day of camp. I had learned a lot of things that would help me get good grades in school and go to Harvard and get a good job someday.

"Tomorrow is Opposite Day," Miss Janey told us before our parents came to pick us up. "So be sure to think backward and do everything opposite tomorrow."

The next day everybody had on backward baseball caps, and they were walking backward and wearing their clothes inside out and stuff like that. We learned lots of new things from Miss Janey. When I grow up, I hope I will be as smart as she is.

At lunch the other kids were complaining, as always.

"I can't wait until the end of the day," Arlo said. "This place is *horrible*."

"We work hard all year long," said

Alexia. "I thought summer was our time to have *fun*."

"We should bust out of this joint," said Michael. "We should get some spoons and use them to dig a tunnel to freedom. Then we could make a break for it. I saw that in a movie once."

"Digging a tunnel would probably take all year," said Ryan. "Camp is over in a few hours."

"What if we used serving spoons?" asked Michael.

That's when a strange thought came into my brain. It was like in the cartoons when a lightbulb appears over someone's head.

Something was terribly wrong.

"What's the matter with *you*?" Arlo

asked me. "Did Somebody steal your encyclopedia?"

"It's Opposite Day," I told him.

"So?"

"So we're supposed to do everything the *opposite* of what we usually do," I said. "That's the rule, right?"

"Yeah, so?" said Neil.

"Well, if we usually do schoolwork here, we have to do the *opposite* of schoolwork today."

"You're right, Andrea!" said Emily.

"So we have to play ball," I told them. "We have to run around outside and go crazy."

"Hey, Andrea's right for once in her life!" Arlo shouted.

"In fact," I continued, "if we follow the rules, it would be wrong to do schoolwork today at *all*. And as you know, I always follow the rules."

"Yeah!" everybody shouted.

After we finished lunch, we went over to the counselor's table to speak with Miss Janey.

"Are you kids ready to do some long division drills?" she asked.

"No!" we all yelled.

"We're not going to do any more drills today," I said.

"Why not?" asked Miss Janey.

"Because it's Opposite Day," I told her. "So we have to do the *opposite* of what we usually do."

"Oh, I don't think you understand," said Miss Janey. "Opposite Day just means we do silly things like walk backward and wear baseball caps backward and—"

I wouldn't let her finish her sentence.

"No," I told her. "We are supposed to do *everything* opposite. That's the rule."

"You don't understand . . . ," said Miss Janey.

"You mean I understand perfectly?" I asked.

If it was Opposite Day, *everything* had to be opposite. Miss Janey looked like she was getting mad.

"You do what I *tell* you to do!" she said, pointing her finger at me.

"Yes, we do the exact *opposite* of what

you tell us to do," I said, pointing my finger back at her. "That's the rule."

"You can't do that!" shouted Miss Janey.

"Oh, you mean it's perfectly fine for us to do that?" I asked.

"Stop!" shouted Miss Janey.

"Start?" I shouted back.

I guess the other kids in the lunchroom were watching us. Because the next thing I knew, they were all stomping their feet and pounding on the tables and chanting.

"Opposite Day! Opposite Day! Opposite Day!"

"Come on, everybody!" I shouted. "Let's go play!"

"Yeah!"

All the kids ran out of the lunchroom together. We spent the rest of the afternoon playing tag and kickball and hide-and-seek without any counselors. It was fun!

★

The #10 reason why I love school . . .
School is fun!

Arlo is always saying he hates reading, he hates writing, he hates math, and he hates school. Arlo says he hates everything. But he never says how much fun we have at Ella Mentry School.

Like the time our custodian, Miss Lazar, had to save Mr. Klutz's life by sticking a toilet bowl plunger on his bald head. Or the time our computer teacher, Mrs. Yonkers, showed us the machine she invented that turns vegetables into junk food. Or the time we made the largest pizza in the world with Mr. Tony, our after-school-program director. Or the time our security guard, Officer Spence, arrested all the teachers and put them in jail. Or the time we got to go on the

time boat, and we traveled back to the
year 1776. I could go on and on.

If I had been sitting home watching
TV and playing video games, I wouldn't
have seen any of these things. That's
why I love going to school. It's fun!

★

A List of Lists

All in all, I really loved Camp Ockatolly-quay. So I added it to my list of things I love. . . .

- Dressing up
- Anything that's pink
- Vanilla ice cream
- Singing
- Shopping

- Making people happy
- Getting compliments (especially from grown-ups!)
- Getting straight As on my report card
- Dancing
- William Shakespeare
- Animals (They don't talk back and say mean things like boys.)
- Reading dictionaries and encyclopedias
- Going to school
- Camp Ockatollyquay

Well, that's the end of my list of reasons why I love school. Isn't making lists fun? I love making lists. Making lists is a great way to keep things organized, and that's really important if you want to become valedictorian and go to Harvard and get ahead in life.

I like making lists so much, I made a list of my top ten favorite lists. . . .

1. My best friends
2. My favorite Cray-Z songs
3. My favorite scarves
4. My favorite Shakespeare plays
5. My favorite things to do on a rainy day
6. My favorite months of the year
7. My least favorite months of the year
8. The months of the year that I don't really care about one way or the other
9. My favorite healthy snacks
10. My favorite school subjects (It's so hard to pick, because I love them all.)

Well, it looks like we reached the end of the book, because we're running out of pages. I hope you liked it. I hope Bermuda doesn't get hit by another hurricane. I hope Arlo will mature in time for our wedding. I hope I learn how to like coffee when I'm a grown-up. I hope Arlo doesn't get gingivitis. I hope I become valedictorian and go to Harvard. I hope everyone compliments me on my back-to-school outfits. I hope Arlo will hold hands with me again. I hope I can go back to Camp Ockatollyquay next summer. I hope I can talk Arlo into playing with my Barbies.

That will be easy!

Back to School, Weird Kids Rule!

MY WeiRd SchooL SpeciaL

WEIRD EXTRAS!

★ Professor A.J.'s History of School Supplies

★ Fun Games and Weird Word Puzzles

★ My Weird School Daze Trivia Questions

★ The World of Dan Gutman Checklist

PROFESSOR A.J.'S HISTORY OF SCHOOL SUPPLIES

Howdy, My Weird School fanatics! This is your old pal Professor A.J. speaking to you from my secret laboratory carved into the side of a mountain at an undisclosed location.*

It's back-to-school time, so I figured this would be the perfect chance to tell you everything I know about THE HISTORY OF SCHOOL SUPPLIES.

Stop! Wait! Don't close the book! This is going to be interesting. I promise.

Seriously, it's really important for you to learn stuff like how pencils are made. Because one of these days, your teacher is going to

—————————————————————

*My bedroom

ask you, "How are pencils made?" and you're going to look like a real dumbhead if you don't have an answer. You don't want to look like a dumbhead, do you?

Okay, here's the scoop—it all started back in ancient Egypt, like so many things did. It was the year 1325 B.C. King Tut was carving some hieroglyphics into a rock one morning when he said, "Man, this stinks! I'm getting carpal tunnel syndrome out here! This sure would be a lot easier if I had a piece of paper and a pencil."

So King Tut took a hunk of wood and a burned stick, and he made the first primitive paper and pencil. Today, of course, pencils are made in a completely different place—Pennsylvania.

Okay, I totally made all that stuff up. There's no way that King Tut would be carving hieroglyphics into a rock. He would have had his servants do it for him! And pencils in Pennsylvania? Man, you'll fall for *anything*! I bet that if I told you rulers come from Rulervania and glue sticks come from Gluestickvania, you would buy it.

But here's some real *true* stuff about school supplies that I just found out. . . .

PENCILS

Pencils have been around for centuries, but it wasn't until 1858 that some guy named Hymen Lipman thought of sticking an eraser on the end of a pencil. Genius! He should have gotten the Nobel Prize for that idea. That's a prize they give out to people who don't have pencils.

Did you know that pencils don't have lead in them? No, they have this stuff called graphite. The average pencil has enough graphite in it to write a line thirty-five miles long. But why would anybody want to do that? Those people must have too much time on their hands, if you ask me.

There are all kinds of pencils, like grease pencils (for slicking back your hair), golf pencils (in case you lose your clubs), and charcoal pencils (which come in handy if you want to write and have a barbecue at the same time).

PENCIL SHARPENERS

Before the invention of the pencil sharpener, people sharpened their pencils with a knife. As you can imagine, there were a lot of accidental stabbings back in those days. Then came some French guy named Eiche Gardner, who invented the first pencil sharpener in 1828. After that, all the kids at school stopped making fun of him because his name was Eiche.* Electric pencil sharpeners came along in 1917. Today, they're probably working on solar- or wind-powered pencil sharpeners. The only problem is that when you want to sharpen a pencil, you'll have to go up on your roof. That could be more dangerous than using a knife.

Still awake? Isn't this interesting? Great! Let's continue. . . .

---

*I have no idea how to pronounce that.

RUBBER BANDS

People have been using rubber bands since 1600 B.C., but they didn't have anything to wrap them around back then, so it was pretty pointless. An Englishman named Stephen Perry patented the modern rubber band, which is used by millions of people all over the world to knock down little plastic army men. Perry woke up one day in 1845 and said to himself, "What should I do today? Cure cancer? Bring about world peace? Or invent the rubber band?"

So he invented the rubber band. Then he went back to bed.

Rubber bands are made from real rubber, which comes from rubber trees. So if you lose a whole bunch of rubber bands and your mom says, "Rubber bands don't grow on trees, you know," you can tell her, "Yes they do."

POST-IT NOTES

Some people call them "sticky notes." But if they're sticky, how come you can pull them right off? That's what I want to know. They should be called notes that *aren't* very sticky.

Actually, Post-it notes were invented by mistake!* In 1968, a scientist named Spencer Silver was trying to develop a super-strong glue. His glue wasn't very strong, but it was perfect for the times when you want a note you can paste on and peel off. Post-it notes come in handy in all sorts of situations, like when you want to see how many of them you can stick to your forehead at one time.

Are you getting all this? Good. There will be a test at the end of the book.**

---

*Hey, you know what would have been cool? If the eraser had been invented by mistake.

**No there won't.

BACKPACKS

You may not believe this, but in ancient times cavemen wore backpacks just like you do. But they didn't carry notebooks and school supplies in them. No, they would hunt their prey and carry it home in a backpack. It's probably not a good idea to put dead animals in your backpack today. Your mom would probably get mad, and it would stink up the house, too.

Isn't this interesting?

CRAYONS

Crayons were invented by ancient Egyptians (Hey, how come *young* Egyptians never invented anything?). They made them out of hot beeswax, and when people came snooping around and asking what they were working on, the Egyptians would say, "None of your beeswax." I've also heard that they used colored pigments in their crayons, but I think that's a pigment of their imagination.

The word "crayon" dates back to 1644, and it means "chalk" and "earth." They should be called crayoffs, if you ask me.

I could tell you a lot more stuff about school supplies, but really, who cares? They're just *school supplies.* It's not like you need to know the history of the Sharpie in order to write with one. I'm sure you have more important things to do than read this junk, anyway. Like pester your parents. Or go to the pool and take one last glorious cannonball off the diving board before the first day of school.

Bummer at the end of the summer!

Now, that wasn't so bad, was it? Think about it—if it weren't for the brave and brilliant men and women who created all these wonderful back to school supplies, we wouldn't—

Hey, wait a minute! If it weren't for *them*, we wouldn't have to go to school in the first place!

I hate school supplies.

Sincerely,

Professor A.J. (the professor of awesomeness)

FUN GAMES AND WEIRD WORD PUZZLES

MATH MIND GAMES

Directions: It's the first day of school, and math is everywhere! Help A.J. and his friends solve these wacky word problems.

1. Andrea has 10 crayons, but, nah-nah-nah boo-boo, A.J. took 5 of them! How many does Andrea have now?

2. A.J. has 2 pairs of socks, but one sneaky sock got lost in the dryer. How many socks does A.J. have now?

3. Mr. Granite's class had 1 snake, and then they bought a hamster, a rabbit, and a fish. How many amazing animals do they have now?

4. There are 12 boys in the class and 9 girls. How many students are there in total?

LOCKER LOOK-ALIKES

Directions: A.J.'s locker is a mess! But Alexia's is even messier. Can you spot the differences between these two pictures? (Hint: There are ten!)

47

BACK-TO-SCHOOL CROSSWORD

Directions: Help A.J. fill in the blanks below with all his favorite school locations, supplies, and activities.

ACROSS

1. What do you use when you make a mistake with a pencil?
2. Where can you go in your school to check out books and do research?

DOWN

1. What instrument do you use to measure length?
2. What game do you play that has four bases, a bat, and a pitcher?
3. What can you do with a book, a newspaper, or a cereal box?
4. Where can you find a slide, a swing set, or a soccer field?

PLAYGROUND PUZZLERS

Directions: Looks like A.J. and his friends had too much fun on the playground—now they're all jumbled up! Rearrange the letters to find out what parts of the playground they were playing on.

1. GUNLEJ YMG _____
2. GINWSS _____
3. ELSDI _____
4. WESEAS _____
5. DASN ITP _____

SCHOOL SUPPLY SHOPPING

Directions: Andrea wants to find the perfect pen for the first day of school. The only problem is she's lost! Help Andrea find the pen aisle in her favorite school supplies store.

CREATIVE CLASSROOMS

Directions: A.J. and Andrea are shopping for their first day of school! Match what cool clothes and super supplies go with each class.

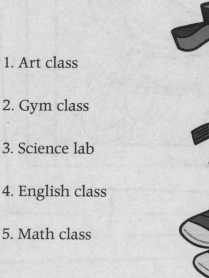

1. Art class

2. Gym class

3. Science lab

4. English class

5. Math class

MY WEIRD SCHOOL DAZE
TRIVIA QUESTIONS

There's no way in a million hundred years you'll get all these answers right. So nah-nah-nah boo-boo on you! (But if you want a hint, all the answers to the questions below can be found in the My Weird School Daze series.)

Q: ACCORDING TO A.J., WHAT DOES PTA STAND FOR?

A: Parents who Talk A lot

Q: HOW MANY BONBONS CAN MRS. DAISY EAT IN ONE SITTING?

A: A whole box!

Q: WHAT KIND OF COSTUME WAS OFFICER SPENCE WEARING AT THE FIRE SAFETY ASSEMBLY?

A: A fireman costume

Q: WHAT DID A.J. GET FOR CHRISTMAS?

A: A calculator.

Q: WHAT'S THE FIRST-PLACE PRIZE IN THE SAND CASTLE CONTEST?

A: A trip to France!

Q: WHAT KIND OF SALTWATER TAFFY DOES A.J. BUY ON THE BOARDWALK?

A: Chocolate taffy. Yum!

Q: WHAT KIND OF PEN DOES A.J. WANT TO BUY WHEN HE'S SHOPPING FOR BORING SCHOOL SUPPLIES?

A: A pen with a laser beam in it. Laser beams are cool!

Q: HOW LONG DOES IT TAKE THE SUN'S LIGHT TO REACH EARTH?

A: Eight minutes

Q: WHERE DID MR. GRANITE ORIGINALLY COME FROM?

A: Neptune, New Jersey

Q: WHAT IS COACH HYATT'S SON'S NAME?

A: Wyatt Hyatt

Q: WHAT POSITION DOES A.J. HOPE TO PLAY IN PEE WEE FOOTBALL?

A: Quarterback!

Q: WHAT SPORT DOES MR. GRANITE PLAY ON HIS HOME PLANET OF ETINARG?

A: Llabtoof

Q: WHAT DOES MS. LAGRANGE NAME HER NEW FOOD?

A: Poodlenasta

Q: WHAT COOL STUFF DOES OFFICER SPENCE CARRY ON HIS BELT?

A: A walkie-talkie, a club, and handcuffs

Q: WHAT BOOK DOES WACKY MR. MACKY READ TO A.J.'S CLASS?

A: *The Happy Bunny*

Q: WHO DOES MRS. JAFEE HIRE AS THE NEW GYM TEACHER?

A: Swami Havabanana

Q: WHO DID MRS. ROOPY DRESS UP AS FOR CIVIL WAR WEEK?

A: Stonewall Jackson

Q: WHAT SNACK DOES MRS. JAFEE FEED A.J. AND HIS FRIENDS IN THE VOMITORIUM?

A: Hardtack

Q: WHAT SCHOOL DO MR. KLUTZ, MS. COCO, AND DR. BRAD WANT TO SEND A.J. TO?

A: Dirk School

Q: WHAT FAVORITE TOY DOES A.J. BRING TO SCHOOL?

A: A Striker Smith action figure

Q: WHEN A.J. HYPNOTIZES ANDREA, WHAT DOES HE TELL HER ABOUT HER FEET?

A: That they smell like rotten cabbage!

ANSWER KEY

MATH MIND GAMES

1. 5
2. 3
3. 4
4. 21

LOCKER LOOK-ALIKES

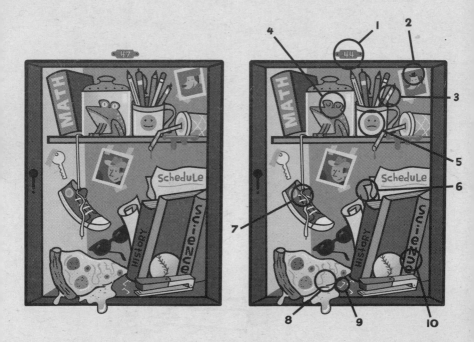

BACK-TO-SCHOOL CROSSWORD

PLAYGROUND PUZZLERS
1. JUNGLE GYM
2. SWINGS
3. SLIDE
4. SEESAW
5. SAND PIT

SCHOOL SUPPLY SHOPPING

PeNs

← FiNiSH →

CREATIVE CLASSROOMS

1.   Art class
2.   Gym class
3.   Science lab
4.   English class
5.   Math class

THE WORLD OF DAN GUTMAN CHECKLIST

MY WEIRD SCHOOL

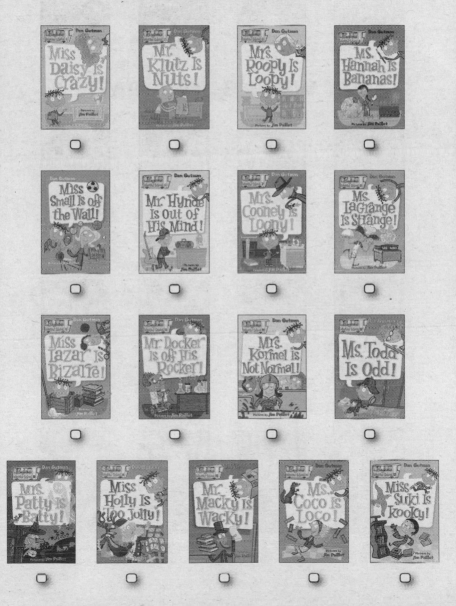

MY WEIRD SCHOOL DAZE

MY WEIRDER SCHOOL

AND CHECK OUT DAN GUTMAN'S WACKY AMERICAN ROAD TRIP SERIES, THE GENIUS FILES